This Walker book
belongs to:

First published 2008 by Walker Books Ltd
87 Vauxhall Walk, London SE11 5HJ

This edition published 2013

2 4 6 8 10 9 7 5 3 1

Text © 2008 Nigel Gray
Illustrations © 2008 Blackbird Design Pty Ltd

The moral rights of the author and illustrator have been asserted

This book has been typeset in FullHouseBrush

Printed in China

British Library Cataloguing in Publication Data:
a catalogue record for this book is available from the British Library

ISBN 978-1-4063-4094-5

www.walker.co.uk

WALKER BOOKS
AND SUBSIDIARIES

LONDON • BOSTON • SYDNEY • AUCKLAND

My Dog, My Cat, My Mum and Me!

NIGEL GRAY

illustrated by

BOB GRAHAM

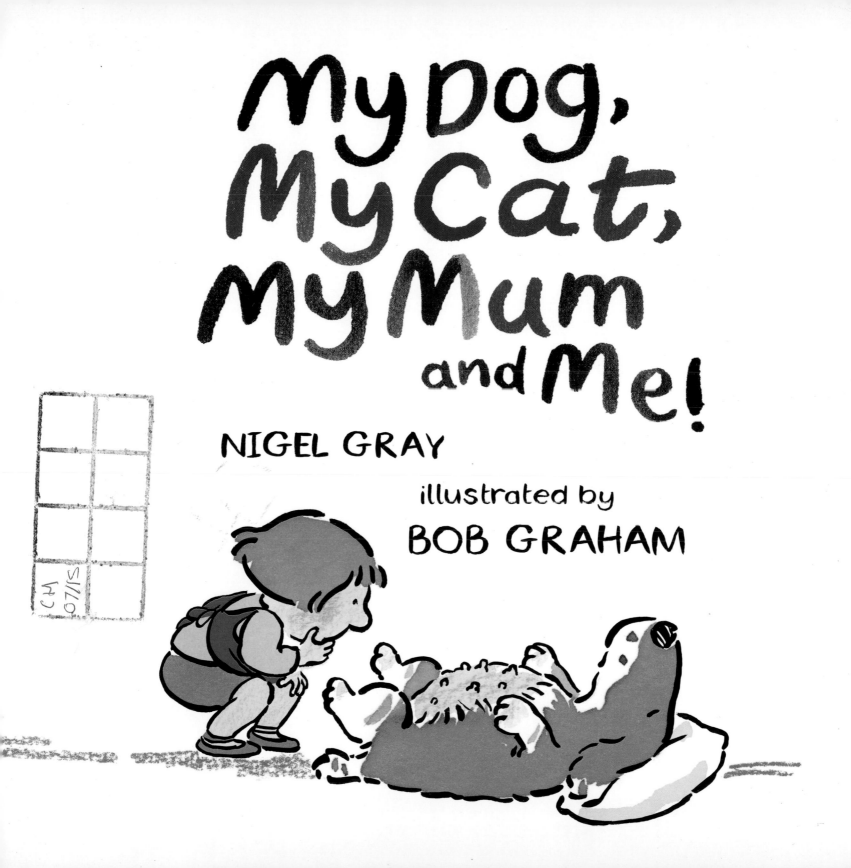

My dog got fatter
and fatter.
I didn't know what
was the matter.

Then do you know what she did?
She went in the cupboard and hid.

She was fat when she went in,
but she came out thin.

I had a peep –
wouldn't you?

My cat got fatter
and fatter.
I didn't know what
was the matter.

Then do you know what she did?
She went in a box and hid.

She was fat when she went in,
but she came out thin.

I had a peep –
what did I see?

My mum got fatter
and fatter.

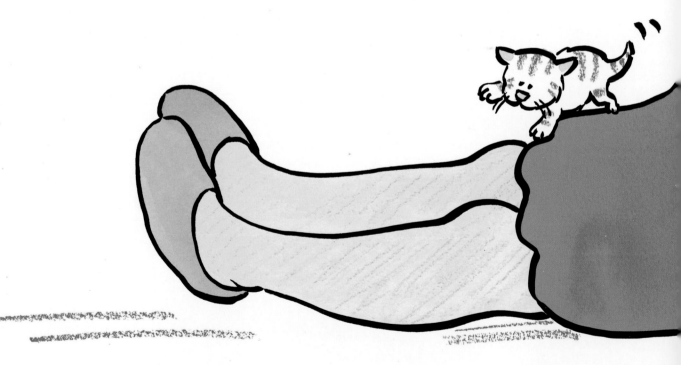

This time I knew what was the matter.

Then do you know what she did?
She called my dad:

"Time for the hospital, Sid!"

She was fat when she went in,
but she came out thin.

I had a peep —
guess what I saw?

NIGEL GRAY

Nigel Gray is an Irish-born award-winning writer, who has written more than sixty books for children. He lives near Perth, Western Australia.

BOB GRAHAM

Bob Graham is one of Australia's finest author-illustrators, whose books have won many awards, including the Kate Greenaway Medal, the Nestlé Smarties Book Prize and CBCA Picture Book of the Year. He lives in Victoria, Australia.

Also by Nigel Gray and Bob Graham:

978-1-4063-4095-2

Other books by Bob Graham:

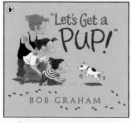 

978-1-4063-0851-8   978-1-4063-2601-7

Available from all good booksellers

www.walker.co.uk